Dear Matthew and
Brooke,
May all of your
dreams come true.

For my lovely and loving family

by Zanita DiSalle
illustrations by Nadine Dennis

Edited by Mary Stafford and Pamela Longhurst

AMETHYST HOUSE
PUBLISHING INC.
www.amethysthouse.com

Sofia's Pink Balloon

by Zanita DiSalle illustrations by Nadine Dennis

There once was a time, not too long ago, when a very special thing happened to a little girl named Sofia.

4

Sofia lived in a house that looked just like a ladybug. It was red with black spots all over. In fact, when people asked Sofia where she lived, she needed only to reply, "ladybug" and everyone knew, right away, what and where she was speaking about.

Sofia liked many things. She liked eating cookies with white icing and rainbow sprinkles. She liked splashing in puddles with her pretty purple rubber boots.

Follow Me To The Fair

She really liked making sand castles at the beach with her big brother. Of all the things that Sofia liked, the one special thing that she liked most of all was pink balloons.

When Sofia heard that the Summer Fair was in her town she asked her big brother to take her there with the hope of finding a pink balloon.

After Sofia and her brother entered the Summer Fair, he told her to be a very good girl and to meet him at the exit of the fair in one hour. Sofia said, "I promise." They gave each other a hug and said a quick good-bye.

Sofia began walking through the fair looking for the balloon man. She looked everywhere, behind the rides and the game booths, but she could not find him. Sofia was just about to ask someone where he was, when suddenly she saw him right in front of her.

He had a long grey beard and large grey whiskers. Balloons of every color seemed to be floating and dancing over his head. He looked something like an old fisherman or a sea captain.

"Excuse me, sir", she said to him. "I would like to buy a pink balloon."

I'm sorry little girl", replied the balloon man, "I have every color, except pink."

Noticing that the little girl looked very disappointed, he thought for a moment before saying, "I should tell you that I do have one very special blue balloon. It is a magical balloon that can turn from a blue balloon into a pink balloon."

"A magical balloon?" whispered Sofia. She quickly gave the man money for the blue balloon. As Sofia walked away she realized, in her excitement she had forgotten to ask the balloon man how the magic worked. When she turned back to ask him, he had disappeared.

Sofia was very clever. She was quite sure that she would be able to figure out the secret of how to change the blue balloon into a pink balloon. She went strolling happily through the Summer Fair with her new magical balloon.

LIVE STOCK

Livestock →

15

Sofia's first plan to change the balloon's color was to tap lightly on the balloon three times and say, "blue balloon, blue balloon, change to pink, blue balloon, blue balloon, change to pink."

Sofia closed her eyes and...

Oh no... It was still a blue balloon!

"Think, think, **think,** how can I make it turn to pink?", thought Sofia. She let out a deep sigh. "That was it!" Sofia tried blowing on the blue balloon hoping that her breath would somehow turn it pink.

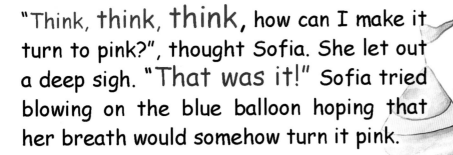

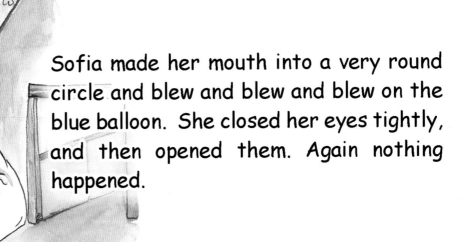

Sofia made her mouth into a very round circle and blew and blew and blew on the blue balloon. She closed her eyes tightly, and then opened them. Again nothing happened.

Sofia was puzzled. She just couldn't find a way to change the blue balloon to pink. She had one last thought, which was to pop the balloon in case the pink balloon was inside the blue one. Just as she was ready to pop the blue balloon she stopped.

Maybe popping the blue balloon wasn't a good idea after all. She realized that if popping the balloon did not work, she would be left with nothing but a broken balloon and that would not be good.

This made her feel very confused. She continued to walk through the fair hoping to find an answer to her problem.

20

By this time Sofia had walked all the way to the end of the fair and it was now almost time to go home.

21

When she was close to the exit of the fair, she heard a boy's voice saying over and over, "One, two, please be true, can you change from pink to blue? One, two, please be true, can you change from pink to blue?"

To Sofia's surprise, she saw that the boy was holding a pink balloon!

Sofia walked over to the little boy and introduced herself, "Hi, my name is Sofia."

"Hi Sofia, my name is Christopher. I have a magical pink balloon and I'm trying to make it turn blue."

"That's funny! I have a magical blue balloon that I'm trying to turn pink."

23

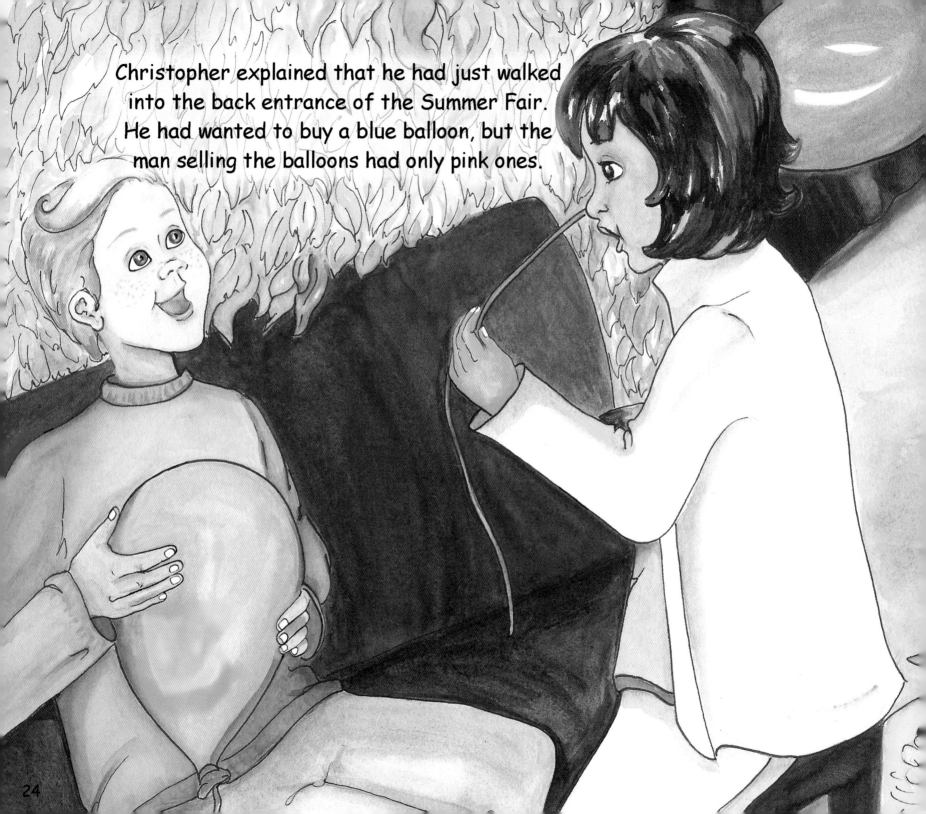

Christopher explained that he had just walked
into the back entrance of the Summer Fair.
He had wanted to buy a blue balloon, but the
man selling the balloons had only pink ones.

24

The balloon man had told him that he had one very special pink balloon that was actually a magical balloon. It was magical because it could somehow turn from a pink balloon into a blue balloon.

"Did your balloon man look like a sea captain?" Sofia asked Christopher. "Yes." replied Christopher.

"That's strange, mine did too!"

"Have you figured out how to change your balloon's color?" asked Sofia.

"No," said Christopher. "I have tried everything but nothing seems to work."

Sofia and Christopher sat on a bench together, and tried to figure out a way to make the balloons change color.

Sofia said, "I guess your balloon man was wrong." Christopher said, "I guess your's was too."

That's when it happened! The two children looked at each other, smiled, jumped to their feet in excitement and yelled,

"We should trade balloons!"

Sofia now had her pink balloon and Christopher had his blue balloon. They had discovered the secret to the magical balloons

Sofia saw her big brother
waiting for her at the exit gate.

"I have to go. My brother is
waiting to take me home."

"Bye Sofia, I hope thatI see you
again."

30

Sofia and her brother walked off together.
Before they were out of sight, she turned
and waved at her new friend Christopher.
They both had magical balloons after all.